Livonia Public Library
ALFRED NOBLE BRANCH
32901 PLYMOUTH ROAD
Livonia, Michigan 48150-1793
(734)421-6600
LIVN #19

Full STEAM Ahead!
Science Starters

The Four Seasons

Alfred Noble Library
32901 Plymouth Rd.
Livonia, MI 48150-1793
(734) 421-6600

Crystal Sikkens

CRABTREE
PUBLISHING COMPANY
WWW.CRABTREEBOOKS.COM

VVV 3 9082 13657 0671

JUN 2 6 2019

Title-Specific Learning Objectives:
Readers will:

- Explain that a cycle is a sequence of events that repeats itself again and again.
- Recognize that Earth's rotation causes seasons, and describe some changes that happen each season.
- Identify information provided by pictures and diagrams, and information provided in text.

High-frequency words (grade one)	Academic vocabulary
after, and, away, can, have, is, it, of, the, to	cycle, Earth, repeat, season, tilted, weather

Before, During, and After Reading Prompts:

Activate Prior Knowledge and Make Predictions:
Have children read the title and look at the cover images. Make a class KWL chart. Fill in the "Know" and "Want to Know" sections. Ask children:

- What season do you see? What do you already know about fall?
- What other seasons do you know? What do you already know about them?
- What do you want to know about the seasons?

During Reading:
After reading pages 6 and 7, stop and ask children to examine the diagram of Earth's rotation. Ask:

- What does the diagram show? What does it help us understand? (Encourage children to look at the Sun's rays and connect to amount of sunlight.)

After Reading:
Fill in the "Learned" section of the KWL chart. Ask:

- What did you learn about each season?
- What did you learn about how Earth turns?

Make child-created anchor charts for each season. Include the time of year the season happens in your area, plant and animal changes, and human changes. Invite children to draw a picture to add to each season's anchor chart (assign seasons to children).

To my wonderful son Jacob John Sikkens, with all my love

Author: Crystal Sikkens

Series Development: Reagan Miller

Editor: Janine Deschenes

Proofreader: Melissa Boyce

STEAM Notes for Educators: Reagan Miller and Janine Deschenes

Guided Reading Leveling: Publishing Solutions Group

Cover, Interior Design, and Prepress: Samara Parent

Photo research: Crystal Sikkens and Samara Parent

Production coordinator: Katherine Berti

Photographs:
iStock: shironosov: p. 6 (bottom)
All other photographs by Shutterstock

Library and Archives Canada Cataloguing in Publication

Sikkens, Crystal, author
    The four seasons / Crystal Sikkens.

(Full STEAM ahead!)
Includes index.
Issued in print and electronic formats.
ISBN 978-0-7787-6188-4 (hardcover).--
ISBN 978-0-7787-6235-5 (softcover).--ISBN 978-1-4271-2254-4 (HTML)

    1. Seasons--Juvenile literature. I. Title.

QB637.4.S55 2019   j508.2   C2018-906153-7
                                 C2018-906154-5

Library of Congress Cataloging-in-Publication Data

Names: Sikkens, Crystal, author.
Title: The four seasons / Crystal Sikkens.
Description: New York, New York : Crabtree Publishing, [2019] |
   Series: Full STEAM ahead! | Includes index.
Identifiers: LCCN 2018056580 (print) | LCCN 2019002019 (ebook) |
   ISBN 9781427122544 (Electronic) |
   ISBN 9780778761884 (hardcover : alk. paper) |
   ISBN 9780778762355 (pbk. : alk. paper)
Subjects: LCSH: Seasons--Juvenile literature.
Classification: LCC QB637.4 (ebook) | LCC QB637.4 .S55 2019 (print) |
   DDC 508.2--dc23
LC record available at https://lccn.loc.gov/2018056580

Printed in the U.S.A./042019/CG20190215

Table of Contents

Crabtree Publishing Company
www.crabtreebooks.com   1-800-387-7650
Copyright © **2019 CRABTREE PUBLISHING COMPANY**. All rights reserved. No part of this publication may be reproduced, stored in a retrieval system or be transmitted in any form or by any means, electronic, mechanical, photocopying, recording, or otherwise, without the prior written permission of Crabtree Publishing Company. In Canada: We acknowledge the financial support of the Government of Canada through the Book Publishing Industry Development Program (BPIDP) for our publishing activities.

Published in Canada
Crabtree Publishing
616 Welland Ave.
St. Catharines, Ontario
L2M 5V6

Published in the United States
Crabtree Publishing
PMB 59051
350 Fifth Avenue, 59th Floor
New York, New York 10118

Published in the United Kingdom
Crabtree Publishing
Maritime House
Basin Road North, Hove
BN41 1WR

Published in Australia
Crabtree Publishing
Unit 3 – 5 Currumbin Court
Capalaba
QLD 4157

Four Seasons

Most places have four **seasons** each year. The seasons follow a **cycle**. A cycle is a set of events that repeat in the same order.

spring

summer

fall

winter

Each season has different weather.
Weather is what it is like outside.
It can be cold, warm, or hot.
It can be rainy or snowy.

The weather is often rainy and warm in the spring.

The weather is often snowy and cold in the winter.

Around the Sun

We have seasons because of the way Earth moves around the Sun. It takes one year for Earth to move around the Sun.

North America

Spring

In spring, our part of Earth begins to be **tilted** toward the Sun.

Summer

We have summer when our part of Earth is tilted toward the Sun. It gets more direct sunlight.

Earth is tilted as it moves. That means parts of Earth get more or less **direct** sunlight at different times of the year. More sunlight means warmer weather.

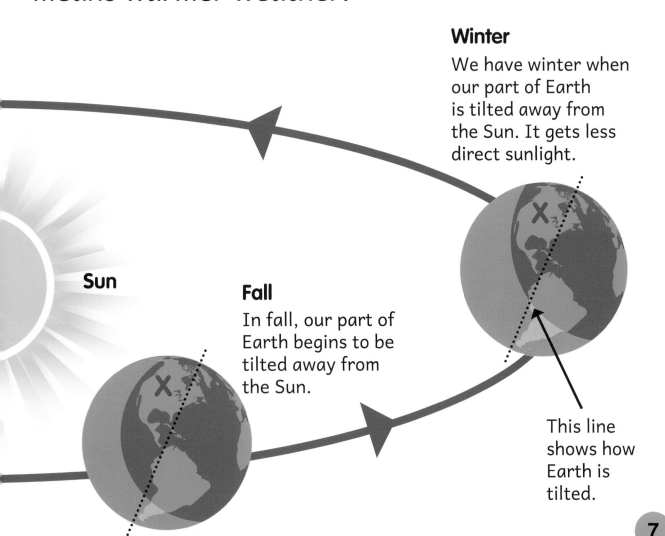

Winter

We have winter when our part of Earth is tilted away from the Sun. It gets less direct sunlight.

Sun

Fall

In fall, our part of Earth begins to be tilted away from the Sun.

This line shows how Earth is tilted.

Hours of Daylight

When the Sun shines during the day, it is called daylight. More sunlight means more hours of daylight too.

There are more hours of daylight in summer, when Earth is tilted toward the Sun.

There are fewer hours of daylight in winter, when Earth is tilted away from the Sun.

Changing with the Seasons

Plants and animals change with the seasons.

Some plants grow fruit, such as peaches, in summer.

Most plants do not grow in winter. Some die. Some grow again in spring.

Animals change to help them **survive** in all types of weather.

Some animals, such as this moose, grow more fur to stay warm in winter.

Animals need to stay cool in summer. Frogs stay cool by covering themselves in mud.

Ready for Winter

Winter is the coldest season. It comes after fall. We do not see many plants outside in winter. It is too cold for them to grow.

Leaves take in sunlight. With less sunlight in winter, many trees do not have leaves.

Food is hard for animals to find in winter. Some animals move to warmer places where there is more food. Some animals, such as bears, sleep through winter.

Barn swallows fly to warmer places in winter.

Groundhogs sleep in **burrows** in winter. They eat a lot of food in fall. The extra food helps them survive.

Set for Spring

Spring is the season after winter. The weather gets warmer. There is more sunlight. This helps trees and plants start to grow again.

Some plants start to grow flowers in spring.

In spring, animals wake up or return from their winter homes. Food is easier for them to find.

Black bears sleep in **dens** during winter. In spring, they wake up and leave their dens. They look for food, such as grass and other plants.

Summer Sun

Summer comes after spring. It is the hottest season. Trees have many green leaves in summer. Flowers grow in all different colors.

There is a lot of sunlight in summer. Sunlight helps plants grow.

Animals change to stay cool in summer. Some spend time in the **shade**. Snakes find shade under rocks.

Some animals, such as red foxes, lose some of their fur in summer. This helps them stay cool.

Time for Fall

Fall is the season after summer. It is also the season before winter. The weather starts to get cool. The leaves on some trees change color and fall off.

The leaves turn from green to yellow, orange, red, and brown.

In fall, animals get ready for winter. Some animals gather food to eat in winter. Other animals start to move to warmer places.

Chipmunks gather food such as acorns in fall. They keep the food in their burrows to eat during winter.

Human Changes

People change with the seasons too. They wear different clothes. They do different outdoor activities.

raincoat

boots

hat

sunglasses

On rainy spring days, people stay dry by wearing raincoats and boots.

In summer, people wear hats and sunglasses to **protect** them from the hot Sun.

How do you change from season to season?

Building a snowman is a fun way to spend a snowy winter day.

In fall, people rake leaves that fall from the trees. They might play in the leaves too!

Words to Know

burrows [BUR-ohs] noun
Holes in the ground dug by animals and used for shelter

cycle [SAHY-kuh l] noun
A set of events that happen again and again, in the same order

dens [dens] noun
Shelters of wild animals

direct [dih-rekt] adjective Describes moving in a straight or short line

protect [pruh-TEKT] verb
To keep from being hurt

seasons [SEE-zuhns] noun Four times of year with different weather

shade [sheyd] noun
Place that is sheltered or kept out of the Sun

survive [ser-VAHYV] verb To stay alive

tilted [TILT-ed] adjective
Slanted or leaning

A noun is a person, place, or thing.
A verb is an action word that tells you what someone or something does.
An adjective is a word that tells you what something is like.

Index

About the Author

Crystal Sikkens has been writing, editing, and providing photo research for Crabtree Publishing since 2001. She has helped produce hundreds of titles in various subjects. She most recently wrote two books for the popular Be An Engineer series.

To explore and learn more, enter the code at the Crabtree Plus website below.

www.crabtreeplus.com/fullsteamahead

Your code is:
fsa20

STEAM Notes for Educators

Full STEAM Ahead is a literacy series that helps readers build vocabulary, fluency, and comprehension while learning about big ideas in STEAM subjects. *The Four Seasons* uses photographs and diagrams to help readers identify and distinguish between the information found in words and in visuals. The STEAM activity below helps readers extend the ideas in the book to build their skills in arts, math, and science.

Art Through the Seasons

Children will be able to:
- Make diagram of a cycle showing the seasons.
- Use a different art form to show each season.

Materials
- Art Through the Seasons Handout
- Animal Tracks Page
- Project materials including crayons, paint, paintbrushes, sponge, leaves, flowers, large book, images of animal prints, poster board, paper, scissors, and glue

Guiding Prompts
After reading *The Four Seasons*, ask:
- How do animals change from season to season? How do plants change?
- Review pages 20 and 21. Can you think of any other ways you change in each season?

Activity Prompts
Explain to children that a diagram is a drawing that shows us how something works or is related. There are diagrams on pages 4, 6, and 7 of this book. They help us understand the seasons.

Tell children that they will use four art forms to make a diagram of the cycle of the four seasons.

Each child gets a copy of the Art Through the Seasons Handout and the necessary materials (see handout). They will create the following:
- Fall: A colorful rubbing of a leaf
- Winter: A symmetrical snowflake
- Spring: A pressed flower, glued to the paper
- Summer: A stamp of animal tracks

Encourage children to think about how each piece of art represents the season. (Animal tracks represent active animals in summer.)

When all of the art is finished, children will cut the paper around each art form into a circle. They will glue the circles, in the form of a cycle, on poster board. They will label each season.

You may choose to create the diagrams together, step by step. Or, review the instructions with children and allow them to create it on their own.

Extensions
- Invite children to create a new way of representing a season of choice, through art.

To view and download the worksheets, visit **www.crabtreebooks.com/resources/ printables** or **www.crabtreeplus.com/ fullsteamahead** and enter the code **fsa20**.